COLOUR JETS

REGGIE the STUNTMAN

Kate Shannon

Collins

COLOUR JETS

First published in paperback in Great Britain by
HarperCollins*Publishers* Ltd 1998

The HarperCollins website address is
www.**fire**and**water**.com

11 10 9 8 7 6 5 4 3 2

Text and illustrations © Kate Shannon 1998

The author/illustrator asserts the moral right to be
identified as the author/illustrator of the work.

A CIP record for this title is available
from the British Library.

ISBN 0 00 675357 4

Printed in Hong Kong

Chapter 1

Hi! I'm Reggie Darroway and I work in the movies. I've been in hundreds of films – but I bet you've never heard of me.

Did you see *Return of the Slime Monster?*
That was one of my films. I was
squashed by the slime
monster and thrown
over a cliff.

Or did you
see *Liberty Day?*

That's me
jumping off
the blazing
alien space
ship. It's all
in a day's
work for a
stunt man.

I may not be famous, but I get my picture taken with all the stars.

When I'm not crashing through windows or falling out of helicopters, I catch up on the latest gossip in *Movie News.*

MOVIE NEWS
IDAHO SMITH – DISASTER MOVIE!

Producer Rathbone D. Hammond caused an uproar in Hollywood today when he once again fired the entire cast and crew from the set of multi-billion dollar action-adventure blockbuster, Idaho Smith Strikes Back. Ex-stars Wayne Zane and Melind Lee were unavaible for commer

This is my cat, Tululah. She's in the movies too. She's what you'd call a stunt cat.

Did you see that ad. where the cat knocked over a really expensive vase?
That was Tululah.

She practised a lot for that stunt.
I haven't got any vases left.

I really hate vases ... oops there goes another one.

Chapter 2

Life between films can be quiet for me and Tululah, but when the phone rings, well, it could be anyone.

Hi Reggie! This is Rathbone D. Hammond. Are you busy? You're gonna love this movie!

Rathbone D. Hammond was calling from his office in L.A. He sounded a bit muffled. I didn't know if it was a bad line or his hay fever – Rathbone's famous for his allergies.

I'm always excited about a new job, but when I heard the name of the film…

Idaho Smith Strikes Back! Oh no! I'm not coming all the way to Los Angeles just to be fired next week.

Original Country Manor House

WILLOUGHBY MANOR HOTEL

Covenient location for Spanglewood Studios

AVAILABLE NOW

"You won't have to, Reggie!" chirped Rathbone. "We've relocated to England."

The effects are out of this world, and Ross Mortimer is the new Idaho Smith.

That'll mean a lot of stunts.

I'd worked with
Ross before –
he wouldn't
risk spoiling
his looks by
doing anything
dangerous.

The new
leading lady
was Jasmine
DeVine – I'd
worked with
her before,
too. Ouch!

There was also the
child star, Kristal
May. She looked
sweet enough, but
who could tell?

STARDUST
EXCLUSIVE
Kristal
May
NEW KID
ON THE
BLOCK
PLUS! MOVIE
GUIDE

11

Come on, Reggie.
Whaddaya say?
There's a hot part
for Tululah...

That was big of
him. I knew he was
allergic to cats, too.

O.K. We'll
take it.

"Kids, animals and Ross Mortimer,"
I smirked, as I hung up. What was I
letting myself in for?

Anyway, that was how it all got started.
Just a phone call.

Chapter 3

Movies – sound glamorous, don't they? Suntan and cocktails… or in this case, crisps and cold tea.

The following week Tululah and I drove to Spanglewood Studios in Bleakshire, where *Idaho Smith* was being shot.

Already things seemed to be going wrong.

Rathbone D. Hammond had just
walked off the set. He'd obviously been
annoying Wacko Schlockberg, the
director, who was flapping his arms
around like a mad hairdresser.

Soon it was our turn to be filmed.

O.K. Reggie and Tululah – jump!

Tululah and I jumped off the roof a few times, then we took a break.

Tululah curled up and took a nap – she's a real pro.

TULULAH

I took a look round the set. A couple of the extras looked familiar, but I'm not very good with faces.

Ross Mortimer was running on the spot to keep warm. When he smiled, his perfect white teeth dazzled the camera.

Kristal, darlin', isn't your mother a great director? I'm just her type of actor don't you think?

Never work with children and adults.

Before Kristal could answer, Ross's mobile phone rang. It was his mother, checking up on him as usual.

Tululah and Kristal seemed to be getting on just fine, so I didn't mind when Kristal started talking to me.

I'd really like to be a stunt girl. Acting is so stupid.

You have to practise a lot, kid.

Kristal, why don't you try jumping off that ten foot wall? It'd be good practice.

Jasmine DeVine had obviously been listening. She gave a glittering smile and walked off. She might be beautiful, I thought, but she's sure got an acid tongue. I had a feeling that this film was going to be no picnic.

Places, everyone!

The next scene was a chase along the set with a big explosion at the end. It was then that things started to go very wrong.

Suddenly all the lights went out. Ross got caught up in a cable and was almost strangled.

Then Jasmine was almost crushed by a falling spotlight.

I tripped over Tululah and landed with my nose in a bunch of cables. Nearby I saw something sparkle.

Strange!

After a bit of fumbling in the dark,
Wacko got the lights back on.

Now I could see what I'd found. It was
an earring! Not one of Jasmine's, but I
was sure I'd seen it somewhere before.

I showed the earring to Kristal and Tululah. Kristal thought it might be a clue to something.

Tululah seemed to be trying to tell me something too, but I just wasn't getting the message.

Chapter 4

That evening we gathered in the huge dining room of Willoughby Manor where we were staying. It was a creepy old place.

What's this?

Elk soup, Sir.

The beady eyes in the paintings seemed to follow us around the room – or maybe we were getting jumpy.

"Trust her to like it," hissed Kristal, who flatly refused to eat. I agreed – I usually brought my own grub to shoots. Baked beans for me, tinned salmon for Tululah.

"Cut the spooky chat – it's giving me a rash," snarled Rathbone.

The rest of the meal was no better and by the end, most of us were still hungry – except for Jasmine.

"Maybe we'd better have an early night," said Wacko.

> Mmmm. I've never had pickled liver before.

"That's the first sensible thing you've said all day," snapped Rathbone, who was still playing with his soup.

> Listen up. Tomorrow I want you all on set at 7.00 a.m. pronto. Don't start without me, you hear?

Chapter 5

The next morning it was freezing and I was still tired. Tululah had spent the night purring in my left ear. It sounded like a road drill.

We all got to the set on time. Then we spent the morning setting things up and waiting for Rathbone to show.

By lunch time, we were all tired of waiting, so we went back to the hotel to shake him awake.

But Rathbone didn't answer his door, nor the phone. It was very strange.

Maybe he was allergic to the soup.

Or maybe he's allergic to you.

I got the pass key from the manager and opened Rathbone's door.

Something's definitely wrong.

The bed hadn't been slept in and all his allergy potions were on his bedside table. We searched everywhere, but there was no sign of Rathbone.

Look at that!

Don't call us. We'll call you.

Kristal's sharp eyes had spotted a note. She really was an observant kid.

We were wondering what to do next when the phone rang - a menacing sort of ring.

"We have Hammond," said a muffled voice. "You will wait for further instructions." Then the caller hung up.

Soon after the phone rang again.

I could tell the next few minutes were going to pass like hours…

Chapter 6

We waited, and waited. Then there was a knock at the door.

Wacko opened the box nervously.

There was no doubt about it – it was Rathbone D. Hammond's pony tail. The kidnappers had cut it off.

There was also a note, written in Rathbone's fussy handwriting.

Help!

I'm feeling real bad. They keep giving me coffee. I'm allergic to coffee. Please do what they say. These guys aren't nice.

Rathbone D. Hammond

Then the phone rang again, making us all jump. It was the kidnappers.

Listen carefully. We want one million dollars in used notes. Put the bag of money in the red tyre in the polar bear pit at Bleakshire Zoo. Do this by five o'clock, or you'll never see your boss again. Understand?

Before anyone could reply, the phone went dead. We looked at each other in horror.

"If they want dollars, they must be American," said Kristal. I agreed with her, but I didn't see how it would help us collect the money.

Everyone was silent.

Then…

We'll have to rescue Rathbone ourselves, just like in the movies.

Pick on someone your own size!

We all stared at her.

"Won't that be a bit dangerous?"
said Ross. Jasmine snorted.

And they were
off again.
I just wished
they'd shut up –
I needed to think.

Then, suddenly, I had an idea!

"Newspaper!" I yelled.
"Quick, Kristal, collect all
the newspapers you can find."

My plan came straight out of a film I
was in once – *The Great Robbery*. The
idea was to cut out rectangles, exactly
the same size and shape as dollar bills.
Then, we'd bundle them together and
put a real dollar on the top of each pile.

Movie News

$1,000,000 DEBT!

Huge losses for Melinda Lee and
Wayne Zane's production company as
latest movie flops. Action man Zane
did all his own stunts but it didn't
stop the movie from bombing . . .

While Kristal and I were working,
Wacko paced up and down the room.

Don't you think
they'll check the money,
Reggie? After all, this is
real – not a film.

"They won't check immediately," I said.
"We'll keep watch and follow whoever
picks up the money. Then we can
rescue Rathbone."

How? I didn't know yet.

Chapter 7

Bleakshire Zoo was a maze.
We wandered past the aardvarks,
the porcupines and the vultures.

Toile... Lions Polar Bears Snakes

ZOO

I could tell Tululah wasn't happy. She didn't like the look of the vultures.

43

At last we found the polar bear pit. The sides were high and, all around, there was a chilly-looking pool.

Right in the middle of the pit was the red tyre. The polar bear was sitting on it.

It's impossible!

Ross, darling, lend me your scarf.

Hey!

"We need to distract the bear," I said.
At once, Kristal started yelling at it.
The bear ignored her.

Nothing's impossible.

Hey! Mr Bear!

Mission Impossible.

Jasmine threw Ross's scarf into the pool.

"Now look what you've done. It'll shrink and go all crinkly," yelled Ross, frantically snatching at it.

Unfortunately he leaned a little too far over the edge...

SPLASSH!!!

Well done, Ross!

The noise caught the bear's attention. It got up from the red tyre and went to investigate the strange new Ross-fish splashing in its pool.

Supper already?

47

In a flash, I vaulted into the pit and
placed the bag of fake money in the tyre.

I got out as quickly as I could, but it
wasn't easy – even for a stunt man.

Luckily, a large crowd had gathered to watch Ross's rescue, so nobody was looking at me.

An important-looking zoo official hoisted Ross out of the pool. The bear looked very disappointed.

Somebody pushed me. I'll probably get pneumonia.

Leaving so soon?

Isn't that Ross Mortimer?

The movie star??

Chapter 8

When all the fuss had died down, we hid behind a nearby tree, wondering what to do next. The zoo would be closing soon – the keeper had already shut the polar bear in his den for the night.

Suddenly Kristal grabbed my arm.
A shadowy figure had appeared from nowhere.

As we watched, he somersaulted into the bear pit and made straight for the red tyre!

Something was bugging me, and it wasn't mosquitos.

We followed the shadowy figure to a block of flats on the outskirts of town. The place was abandoned, except for a light shining from a window on the seventh floor.

53

On the seventh floor, Tululah, Wacko and I went into the flat next to the kidnappers, while Kristal, Ross and Jasmine guarded the door.

True – I wasn't on set now, but I'd done a stunt like this in my last film.

I tucked Tululah into my jacket, took a deep breath and jumped.

Seconds later, Kristal and Jasmine burst through the front door and a huge fight broke out.

Err – I'll go and phone the police.

I knew I would have been purrfect in *The Jungle Book*.

Tululah really got her claws into the action.

Then, suddenly, it was all over.

Amazingly, Jasmine had flattened both kidnappers with her handbag.

Kristal stepped over the dazed kidnappers and pulled the plaster from Rathbone's mouth.

Thanks, guys. Do you know they've cut off my pony tail? How could they be so cruel...?

"Maybe it's not so surprising after all," I said. "Not when your kidnappers are..."

"It all added up," I said. "It had to be someone with a grudge, who needed money…"

"That earring you lost had me foxed – until I remembered where I'd seen it before," I told Melinda.

"And that somersault you did at the zoo was the one you do in all your films, Wayne."

You left a trail of clues a mile long!

Pah! Actors!

Chapter 10

Next day, the rescue of Rathbone D. Hammond was front page news.

DAILY DRONE

FILMSTAR IN DARING RESCUE

Daring film star Ross Mortimer in real-life rescue of famous Hollywood producer, Rathbone D. Hammond.

Somehow, Ross had managed to get all the credit for the rescue.

Yes Mother, I'm a hero.

Mortimer, you're a dirty, rotten fake!

Kristal and Tululah took it all in their stride – they spent the day practising stunts as if nothing had happened.

It was all too much for Wacko, however. He decided to give up film directing and take up hairdressing.

We call this style 'the director's cut'.

It didn't take long for Rathbone to recover from the kidnap and start giving orders again.

I just smiled.

Forget Idaho Smith, Reggie. My rescue would make a great movie! Now, who could we get to play you...?

As long as it's not Ross Mortimer...

That's life, being a stunt man.

You don't even get to star in your own film.